JUMP!

ANDREW PLANT

FORD ST

When the littlest Quig hatched in the Cloud Tower,
the first thing he saw was the whole city,
spread out below him.

One by one, his brothers and sisters rolled
out of their eggs, creeping up to the edge
with their sticky fingers, and staring.

The other Quigs learnt to climb quickly,
scampering up and all over the tower,
fearlessly jumping,

swinging on their clever tails,
and steering with their
powerful fins.

But the littlest Quig didn't join in.

He couldn't jump like the others.

His tail was stumpy and not at all clever.
His fins were thin and wrinkly.
And he was afraid of the huge empty spaces
of the Cloud Tower.

He watched sadly as the others
whooped and laughed
as they swung through the sky
on their tails.

'Hey, Stumpy!' they jeered.
'Why don't you jump like us?
Are you *scared*?
What sort of a Quig are you
if you're scared?'

When the other Quigs leapt and swung
and jumped from tower to tower,
Stumpy began the long climb down

into the shadowy streets

far below.

One day a Poringo
leant down to him.

'What are you doing
down here?' she asked.
'You belong up in the towers.'

But Stumpy didn't feel that he belonged
up there at all.

By the time Stumpy
climbed all the way back up
to where the other Quigs
had been playing,

they had already
left for home.

Day by day, the Quigs became bolder, more daring,
jumping further . . . and further.

'Jump!' they cried to Stumpy.
'Jump! Jump!'

And then they laughed.
They laughed at his stumpy tail.
They laughed at his wrinkly fins.

'You're just so *different*!'
snarled the biggest of the Quigs.
'You don't belong here.
You don't belong with us.
Why don't you just stay down in the dark
where you *do* belong!'

And then they all laughed again,
and swung away on their clever tails.

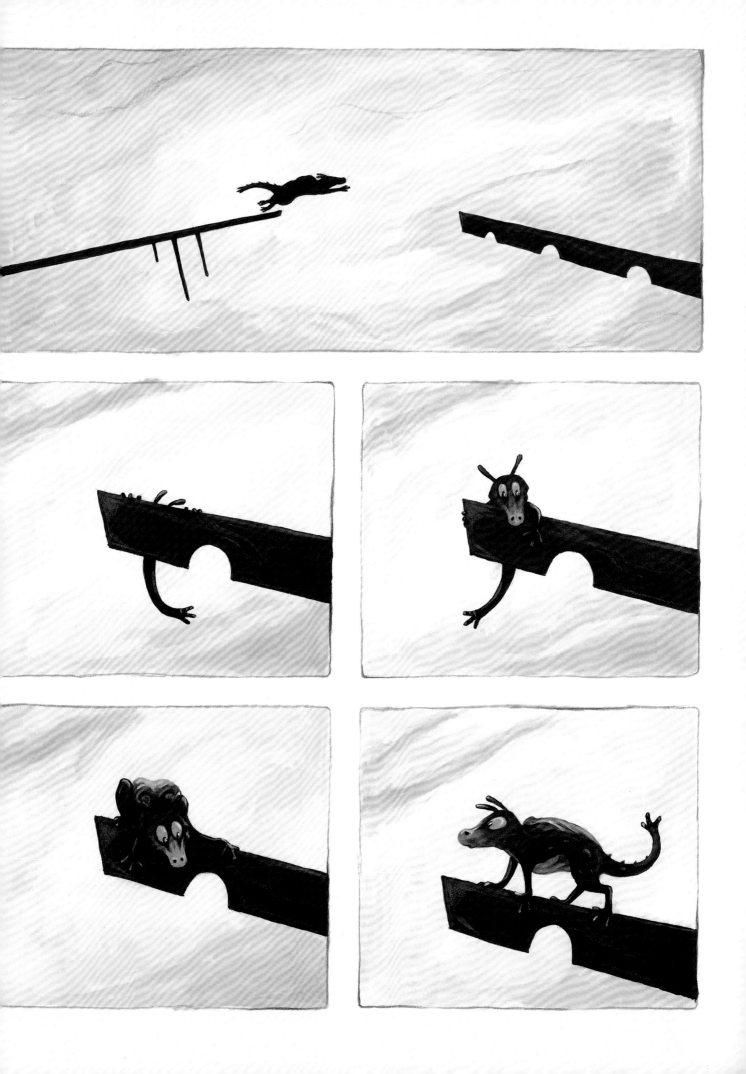

One bright morning,
Stumpy sat on the edge,
breathing hard,
his fingers gripping tight.

The other Quigs were already
whirling and spiralling
around the tower.

'Jump!' called out one as he leapt past.

'He can't!' laughed another.

'Jump!' they both called.

So he did.

Stumpy lived in the Cloud Tower.
All the other Quigs spent their days
jumping high above the city.

Stumpy didn't join them.
Why just jump . . .

...when you can

FLY!

For everyone who has
ever felt that they don't fit in —
we make the world interesting!
— AP

First published by Ford Street Publishing, Melbourne,
Victoria, Australia

2 4 6 8 10 9 7 5 3 1

ISBN: 9781925804454 (hardcover)
ISBN: 9781925804461 (paperback)

Ford Street website: www.fordstreetpublishing.com
First published 2020

A catalogue record for this
book is available from the
National Library of Australia

Design & layout: Cathy Larsen Design

Printed in China by Tingleman Pty Ltd